REVENGE
OF THE
KILLER
VEGETABLES

REVENGE OF THE KILLER VEGETABLES

Written and illustrated by
Damon Burnard

RED FOX

To Nicholas, Georgia and Jessica

A Red Fox Book

Published by Random House Children's Books
20 Vauxhall Bridge Road, London SW1V 2SA

A division of Random House UK Ltd
London Melbourne Sydney Auckland
Johannesburg and agencies throughout the world

Copyright © 1994 by Damon Burnard

1 3 5 7 9 10 8 6 4 2

First published by Andersen Press Limited 1994

Red Fox edition 1996

Printed and bound in Great Britain by
Cox & Wyman Ltd, Reading, Berkshire

RANDOM HOUSE UK Limited Reg. No. 954009

Papers used by Random House UK Limited
are natural, recyclable products made from wood grown in
sustainable forests. The manufacturing processes conform to
the environmental regulations of the country of origin.

ISBN 0 09 942791 5

Chapter 1

It was a quiet Saturday afternoon.

I was busy in my room, working on my costume, when suddenly . . .

'Oh no!' I sighed.

I looked out of the window. Dad was arguing with our neighbour, Mrs Weeny, over the garden fence.

'Why don't you two just wait for the judge to decide tomorrow?' I yelled.

Tomorrow was a very important day in Kaleshill. For on that day, over four hundred years ago, the village was founded by my ancient ancestor, Walter Herbert Kale.

Walter Herbert Kale lived in London during the reign of Queen Elizabeth the First. He was a very famous actor; from Blackheath to Hampstead Heath, everyone knew his name.

He wasn't famous for his stirring speeches and amusing asides, however. Walter Herbert Kale was famous for being the worst actor anyone had ever seen.

He was so bad that the audience pelted him with rotten vegetables during every performance.

One evening he was so incredibly, fantastically, astronomically bad, he was chased out of the city gates by a band of angry theatre critics.

'Fools!' he raged, as he trudged into the countryside.

He was so cross, he buried his vegetable-covered cloak on top of a hill, and sat down in a terrible sulk.

Hour after hour, day after day, week after week he sulked. Meanwhile, the vegetable seeds that had stuck to his cloak started to grow. The soil on the hill must have been very good, because those tiny seeds became the biggest, most beautiful vegetables in the whole wide world.

Walter Herbert Kale, of course, was too busy sulking to notice. But that soon changed when passers-by pressed gold coins into his hand, in exchange for the vegetables. They tasted as good as they looked and before long chefs travelled from far and wide to purchase them.

Walter Herbert Kale was delighted. He hired some helpers and raised more vegetables. Before long, a prosperous little village grew up around the hill.

That hill is now the village green, and the village is called Kaleshill, after Walter Herbert Kale. He was loved and respected by all – until, that is, he built a theatre there.

On opening night, it mysteriously burned down, halfway through his performance of *Hamlet*.

Now, on the same day every year, we dress up as vegetables and march through Kaleshill to celebrate its birthday. Last year I went as a courgette. This year, because I'd grown a little, I was allowed to go as a marrow. A gardening contest took place after the procession, and was taken very, very seriously.

It had always been won by a descendant of Walter Herbert Kale.

Some previous winners of the Kaleshill gardening contest

George Fitzherbert Kale. winner 1770-1781

Victoria Charity Kale. winner 1887-1900

Dad. winner 1980-?

Chapter 2

Dad stormed into the kitchen.

Dad always calls me Curly, even though it's not my real name and my hair's not curly, either. He calls me Curly because my last name is Kale, and Curly Kale is a vegetable a bit like a cabbage. For some reason, Dad thinks that's funny. Just then, though, he was very upset.

'Never mind, Dad!' I said. 'You've won it for as long as anyone can remember. So what if someone else wins for a change?'

'But they can't!' howled Dad. 'It's always been won by a Kale!'

I'd never be able to show my face, if I was the first ever Kale to come second!

Well, there's nothing you can do about that! The contest is tomorrow!

Suddenly, Dad's eyes lit up.
'I know!' he said. 'I'll cheat!'
'Cheat? But you *can't*! It's not fair!'

'Nonsense, Curly!' whispered Dad.

He started rummaging around in the big trunk where he kept all the stuff from his days in the merchant navy.

He snatched up a dusty old chilli-pepper. It was covered with strange writing.

Chapter 3

Suddenly Dad was clattering around
the kitchen, fumbling with funnels
and pestles and herbs and powders.

I didn't want to, but I couldn't help
myself.

'Well, Curly . . . In the Scallion Sea, seventy leagues south of Kuppatee, there lies an island. The last inhabitant of the island gave me this pepper. Written on it is the recipe for a potion that makes vegetables grow to an *incredible* size!'

'The last inhabitant?' I asked.

I watched while Dad whizzed around the kitchen like a crazy whirlwind. All afternoon he heated . . .

mixed . . .   poured . . .

and stirred.

By late evening, he was triumphant.

'IT IS DONE!' he shouted.

In his hand was a small jar, filled with a bubbling liquid.

Dad tiptoed into the garden and carefully dropped a teaspoon of potion onto each vegetable.

'A little is enough!' he whispered.

I don't want to overdo it!

Nevertheless, he dropped an extra teaspoon of potion onto one large potato plant.

Ha! That'll teach Weeny not to be rude about my spuds!

DAD! LOOK!

Before our eyes, the vegetables began to throb and glow.

'I do! Hee, hee, hee!' Dad giggled, rubbing his hands with glee.

I left Dad gloating in the garden and went back up to my room. Carefully I put the finishing touches to my costume.

Before I went to bed, I tried it on. I was delighted. It looked great.

Chapter 4

Early next morning, Dad's angry voice woke me up.

I ran downstairs and into the garden, where Dad and P.C. Stout were standing over the vegetable patch.

It was empty!

'It was YOU!' Dad yelled over the fence at Mrs Weeny.

'THAT'S ENOUGH!' interrupted P.C. Stout. 'This is a serious case of missing vegetables!'

I was furious.

I snatched up the potion.

'Oh no you don't!' I snarled.
'Hasn't it done enough damage
already?'

'Curly! WAIT!'

As hard as I could I hurled the jar
out of the kitchen window.

It sailed through the air, then . . .

it shattered into a zillion pieces on the
patio!

Chapter 5

'I'm sorry, Curly!' said Dad, after he'd calmed down. 'I know how much the procession meant to you! But this is all that thieving Mrs Weeny's fault!'

'How can you say that when you have no proof? Perhaps she has an alibi?' I said.

I stormed up to my room.

I wasn't interested in Dad's apologies, so I turned up the volume on my personal stereo to drown out his voice.

After some thought, I decided that the only thing to be done was to make Dad own up to cheating. What's more, I'd take him to the police station myself.

The trouble was, I couldn't find him anywhere. He wasn't in his room – I even checked under the bed!

He wasn't in the kitchen, either. Or watching TV.

I knocked on her door.

There was no reply.

I looked all around me.

In the distance, I could see a group
of vegetables making their way
towards the village green.

Chapter 6

Quicker than you can say 'Jack Robinson's ridiculous rat, Rodney', I ran home and pulled on my marrow suit.

I rushed off to join the other vegetables, rehearsing the parade's traditional song as I went.

By the time I got there, the green
was crowded with giant vegetables.

'The costumes are really good this
year!' I said to a leek standing nearby.

A huge potato stepped forward.
From its size I guessed that Mrs
Mayor, the Mayor, was inside.

I tried to join in, but the words were
different from the ones I knew.

'Comrades!' the potato roared.

'These aren't my fellow villagers at all!' I gasped.

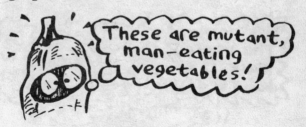

Chapter 7

Amid the uproar, I slipped away. I tore off my marrow suit and ran through the village, hammering on doors and banging on windows.

Standing outside the police station
was P.C. Stout!

'Help!' I screamed, running up to him.

P.C. Stout laughed.

As we walked into the police station
I took a closer look at P.C. Stout.

Even though it was a warm day, he
was wearing an overcoat and a big
scarf.

'Aren't you well?' I asked.

Suddenly . . .

42

I turned on my heels. There, locked in a cell, was Dad.

This came as no great surprise, but with him was everyone else from the village . . .

including P.C. Stout in his underwear!

I turned back to the policeman.

Slowly he pulled off his helmet.

Chapter 8

I was locked in the cell!

'POTION?' squawked Mrs Weeny.

Dad looked at his feet.

'What exactly did happen to the tribe which gave you the recipe?' I asked.

'They were, erm, eaten,' said Dad.

'So this is all your doing!' howled Mrs Weeny. 'And now we're all going to die!'

'Don't get your knickers in a twist!'
said Dad.

'Soon?' demanded P.C. Stout.

Everyone sighed with relief.

Everyone groaned with despair.

'You cad!' the vicar hissed, placing his hands around Dad's throat. Suddenly the police station door opened.

In swaggered a plump, glossy aubergine.

The broccoli and aubergine turned to us.

Chapter 9

First, the broccoli prodded P.C. Stout.

Next, the aubergine poked Mrs Weeny.

Then they both looked at me!

I was marched out of the police station . . .

. . . and up to a huge pot of boiling water on the village green!

I decided to try and stall them.

Suddenly . . .

a monstrous turnip snatched me up!

The turnip growled. It dangled me
over the bubbling pot.

'Vegetable-ist!' the turnip snarled.

I shut my eyes tight and waited for
the drop.

I waited. And waited. I heard the turnip gasp.

A cabbage screamed.

I opened one eye.

I couldn't believe it, so I opened the other.

Chapter 10

Slithering towards us was a snail. But this wasn't just any snail.

This was a gargantuan, gigantic, gruesome snail!

'The potion!' I thought, recalling
how I'd thrown it out of the kitchen
window.

The snail must've drunk
the last teaspoonful
when it shattered
on the
patio!

The snail drew closer, leaving a trail
of sticky slime in its wake.

It looked hungry.

roared President Potato.

shrieked the turnip. It threw me
aside and tipped over the steaming
pot.

The snail fought back fiercely.

The battle raged.

I saw my chance.

Taking advantage of the din and confusion, I made a dash for the phone box at the bottom of the hill. I had to tell someone, somewhere what was going on!

I was nearly there when the broccoli spotted me.

A snarling pack of savage sprouts raced after me.

I ran as fast as I could, but they were gaining on me all the time!

I reached for the phone box door, when suddenly . . .

I slipped on the sprouts swarming and snapping at my feet!

The ground was trembling all around me.

Hurtling down the hill towards me
was the giant turnip!

I couldn't move.
It thundered nearer and nearer
before taking a mighty leap . . .

And then . . .

Chapter 11

Lying on my tummy was a turnip the size of . . . a turnip!

Cautiously I walked back up the hill.
Scattered about were dozens of
vegetables . . .

mounds of gooey slime . . .

and one garden snail that fitted in
the palm of my hand.

The potion wore off just in time!

I spotted P.C. Stout's uniform on the ground. Lying on top was the same stick of broccoli that had arrested me moments before!

I grabbed a bunch of keys from the belt, ran to the police station and unlocked the door.

'Three cheers for Curly, Liberator of Kaleshill!' shouted Mrs Mayor.

'Down with Mr Kale!' hissed Mrs Weeny.

'Ahem! Time I was going!' Dad muttered, but before he could make it through the door, Mrs Mayor grabbed him.

'Well, well, well, Mr Kale!' she said.

'The stocks!' shrieked Mrs Weeny.

'Now calm down, Mrs Weeny!' said P.C. Stout. 'Unfortunately that's not the way we do things these days!'

After much thought and discussion, it was finally agreed. Dad's punishment was to tidy up the mess he'd caused, which meant picking up all the vegetables and shovelling up the snail-slime.

Meanwhile, Mrs Mayor held a party in my honour. What's more, everyone decided to go ahead with the procession the next day . . . with me at its head!

I was going to wear my marrow suit after all!

Meanwhile...

Chapter 12

It was nearly dark by the time the party ended.

I decided to see how Dad was getting on.

He grimly loaded a shovelful of slime onto the brimming wheelbarrow.

Despite everything, I felt sorry for him. To be helpful I began piling up the vegetables that were lying around.

'Thanks, Curly!' said Dad. 'You were right all along. Nothing good comes from cheating.'

I picked up the leek and the aubergine and tossed them onto the pile.

I thought hard.

Suddenly I remembered how Dad had given one of the potato plants a double-dose of potion.

'It's still out there somewhere!' I cried.

'Hey, Curly! Relax!' said Dad. 'The double dose will have worn off by now!'

'I hope you're right this time, Dad!' I said.

'Don't worry,' said Dad.

'Anyway,' Dad said, 'as soon as we've finished here, I'm going to destroy it.'

SMASH!

Come on, Curly! Let's go home and put an end to this whole business!

You know what...

80

Other great reads ✏ *from* **Red Fox**

Further Red Fox titles that you might enjoy reading are listed on the following pages. They are available in bookshops or they can be ordered directly from us.

If you would like to order books, please send this form and the money due to:

ARROW BOOKS, BOOKSERVICE BY POST, PO BOX 29, DOUGLAS, ISLE OF MAN, BRITISH ISLES. Please enclose a cheque or postal order made out to Arrow Books Ltd for the amount due, plus 75p per book for postage and packing to a maximum of £7.50, both for orders within the UK. For customers outside the UK, please allow £1.00 per book.

NAME_____

ADDRESS_____

_____

Please print clearly.

Whilst every effort is made to keep prices low, it is sometimes necessary to increase cover prices at short notice. If you are ordering books by post, to save delay it is advisable to phone to confirm the correct price. The number to ring is THE SALES DEPARTMENT 0171 (if outside London) 973 9000.

Other great reads from **Red Fox**

Discover Red Fox Read Alones – for young readers

MORRIS MACMILLIPEDE – THE TOAST OF BRUSSELS
SPROUT by Mick Fitzmaurice
Morris Macmillipede has a dream. With all his heart and soul
he wants to be the world's first ballet-dancing millipede. Will his
dream come true . . .?

ISBN 0 09 942781 8   £2.99

CABBAGES FROM OUTER SPACE by Lindsay Camp
Emma is a computer game fanatic so when her uncle buys her a
MiniMax Double-X Personal Entertainment System she's in
computer game heaven! She's so hooked on zapping cosmic
cabbages in Ultra Galactica, she doesn't notice when she's
'wobbled' aboard a real alien spacecraft . . .

ISBN 0 09 942771 0   £2.99

THE SALT AND PEPPER BOYS by Jean Wills
When Michael spends a summer at the Seaview Ghost House
he finds a new friend, Lenny, and they become the Salt and
Pepper boys. Together they have a summer of adventure and
seaside fun!

ISBN 0 09 942761 3   £2.99

WILFRED'S WOLF by Jenny Nimmo
Fed up with snowy Scandinavia, a wolf sets off to England in
search of excitement and adventure. Lucky for him he meets
Wilfred, a chef with a soft spot for wolves . . .

ISBN 0 09 930141 5   £2.99

CAT'S WITCH AND THE WIZARD by Kara May
When a wizard comes to the village, all Aggie the Witch's
customers start going to see him instead of Aggie because he has
the latest hi-tech spells and equipment. Aggie and Cat vow to
uncover the wizard as the trickster he really is!

ISBN 0 09 942751 6   £2.99